# Annie Pitts, Artichoke

# Annie Pitts, Artichoke

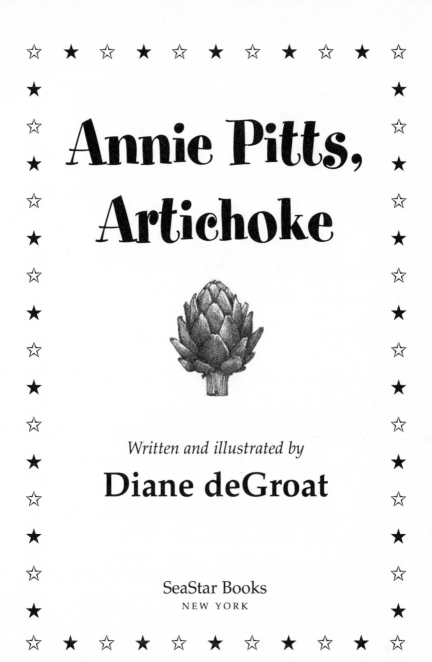

Written and illustrated by

## Diane deGroat

SeaStar Books

NEW YORK

SEASTAR BOOKS
a division of NORTH-SOUTH BOOKS INC.

First published by Simon & Schuster Books for Young Readers, 1992.
Published in 2001 in the United States by SeaStar Books,
a division of North-South Books Inc., New York.
Published simultaneously in Canada, Australia, and New Zealand by
North-South Books, an imprint of Nord-Süd Verlag AG, Gossau Zürich, Switzerland.

Library of Congress Cataloging-in-Publication Data

deGroat, Diane.
Annie Pitts, artichoke / written and illustrated by Diane deGroat
p. cm.
Summary: When Annie and her third grade class put on a play about nutrition,
it has more surprises than the teacher expected.
[1. Schools—Fiction. 2. Nutrition—Fiction. 3. Plays—Fiction.]  I. Title.
PZ7.D3639   An   2001   [E]—dc21     00-10413

The art for this book was prepared using pencil.
The text for this book is set in 13-point Palatino.

ISBN 1-58717-042-6 (RTE)
1   3   5   7   9   RTE   10   8   6   4   2
ISBN 1-58717-043-4 (PB)
1   3   5   7   9   PB   10   8   6   4   2

Printed in the U.S.A.

For more information about our books, and the authors and artists who create them,
visit our web site: www.northsouth.com

# Contents

✯ ✯ ✯

# Miss G. and Me

Blah, blah, something, something, blah, blah . . ."

The teacher went on blah-blahing about something-something, while I just stared out the window, watching a dog on the playground. He had stopped to sprinkle on the monkey bars. I would have to remember not to climb on that side of the monkey bars at recess. I would also have to remember to tell everyone else not to climb on that side.

Everyone except Matthew, that is. I would tell him *after* he did.

When the dog wandered off, I stared at my reflection in the glass. I tilted my head and practiced smiling. I practiced smiling every chance I got, because someday I was going to be a movie star and I would have to smile a lot for the camera.

I would also have to cry a lot. I made a frown in the glass and tried to think of something sad. I thought about the time my hamster died. I was about to cry, really, but then I saw Matthew's reflection behind mine. He was making silly faces. It's so hard to be a serious actress when someone is making silly faces behind you.

Matthew's reflection suddenly disappeared, because something large came between us. It was Miss Goshengepfeffer. "Earth to Annie Pitts!" she said.

I turned around and said, "Sorry, Miss G."

Miss Goshengepfeffer was nice enough to let us call her Miss G., but she was not nice enough to let us daydream in class. It was the beginning of the school year, and I was still in my summer mode. It was hard to pay attention.

Miss G. returned to the front of the room. "As I was saying," she said, looking my way, "the play will be for your parents and for the rest of the school, too. We'll write it together, and everyone will have a part."

*Play?* Did I, Annie Pitts, future star, hear that magic word, *play*? My best friend, Sara, and I used to put on plays in her backyard. We charged kids a quarter to see them, which was really a bargain. I mean, an arcade game costs a quarter, and it can be over in less than a minute. Our plays went on for hours.

Since Sara moved away this past summer,

I hadn't had a chance to do any serious acting, so I suddenly paid very close attention to what Miss G. was saying.

"We can start working on the play at the end of our new science unit," she said. "But first I'd like to tell you about the class trip that's coming up."

I wanted to hear more about the play, but everyone else wanted to hear about the trip. Last year her fourth-graders went to a baseball game. I heard that Miss G. ate ten hot dogs! I believed it, because Miss G. is . . . well, you know.

Thomas raised his hand. "Are we going to a baseball game?"

Miss G. said, "No, we're not going to a baseball game, but we *are* going someplace interesting. And you've probably been there before."

"I went on a trip to Disney World this summer," Thomas said.

Disney World? I'd love to go to Disney World! Maybe I could try out for a part in a Disney movie if we went there. I was daydreaming again, thinking about which stage name I preferred, Tiffany or Brooke, while Miss G. was writing something on the board: SUPERMARKET.

Supermarket? What has that got to do with Disney World, I wondered. And then I realized: we weren't going to Disney World. No Fantasyland. No chance to be a movie star. We were going . . . food shopping! That was not my idea of a class trip.

I guess I wasn't the only one who didn't think so. Thomas asked, "Why are we taking a trip to the supermarket? I've been there plenty of times."

I found that hard to believe, because Thomas's family had a housekeeper who did all the shopping for them. I couldn't imagine Thomas, or even Thomas's mother, in the supermarket trying to decide between the floral- or the pine-scented room spray.

"The supermarket can be very interesting," Miss G. said. "Our new science unit is about nutrition. We're going to do a play about it, but first we'll learn about making healthy choices in our diet. And all the different foods we'll be discussing can be found right in our local supermarket."

Miss G. wrote NUTRITION on the board. I didn't copy it on the paper in front of me when she asked us to. Instead, I wrote M-I-C-K-E-Y M-O-U-S-E.

"Now, who can name some good foods?" Miss G. asked, chalk in hand.

Marsha said, "Ooh, ooh," and waved her arm. Obviously, Marsha-Miss-Pick-Me-Pick-Me wasn't very upset about not going to Disney World. "Chocolate!" she said. "Chocolate is good."

"Chocolate is very good," Miss G. said.

"And so are doughnuts and cookies. But they're not good *for* us. We need to eat foods that have things like . . . protein." She wrote the word on the board. "Meat, fish, chicken, and eggs are all sources of protein. Beans and nuts have it, too."

I looked over at Matthew, looking over at me, making nutty faces. If nuts had protein, then Matthew must have more protein than anyone else in the class.

Miss G. drew a huge circle on the board. She drew a fork on one side and a knife and spoon on the other. Then, for some reason, she drew a guitar right in the middle of the circle.

"Now we need some vegetables, a dairy product, and maybe a cereal or pasta. That will give us a balanced meal." She looked at me and said, "Annie, what vegetable shall we put on our plate?"

I was still staring at the guitar. "Plate?" I asked.

"Here, next to the chicken," she said. "I guess I'm not a very good artist." She wrote the word CHICKEN on the guitar. I mean, on the chicken.

"Well, Annie?" she continued. "What vegetables would you like?"

"I don't like vegetables," I said very matter-of-factly. And that was true. I always left them on my plate. But I could probably learn to like them in Disney World.

Miss G. was not giving up so easily. "Annie," she said, "we can all learn to eat right even if there are certain foods we don't like."

Before I could stop myself, I said, "Do YOU eat right, Miss G.? I mean, how come you're so . . . so . . ."

Some kids giggled. Marsha-Miss-I'm-So-Polite gave me a look that said, "How could you?"

But Miss G. wasn't mad. She said, "You're right, Annie. I don't always eat properly, as you can see." She patted her hip. "I just love sweets. Cake, ice cream, cookies, *chocolate*!" She sighed a little before going on. "But I've started a new diet this year, and this time I'm going to eat right. I'm going to set a good example for my students."

We all agreed that Miss G. should lose some weight. And we would help her. Matthew said that he would check her desk each morning to make sure that she wasn't sneaking in doughnuts. Thomas suggested that she take karate lessons. Marsha suggested that I keep my mouth shut.

# The Trip to You-Know-Where

Before the class trip, Miss G. gave us a talk about proper behavior. I already knew how to act in a supermarket, but maybe some kids didn't. I once saw a little boy throw a tantrum when his mother wouldn't buy him candy. Maybe Miss G. was afraid one of us might do the same. Maybe she thought it would be me.

As we headed out the door, Miss G. said, "Don't forget your nutrition charts. You have to write examples of all the different food groups on it." My chart had M-I-C-K-E-Y M-O-U-S-E written across the top. But that didn't change the fact that this trip was going to be pretty B-O-R-I-N-G.

When we lined up in front of the school, five cars were already waiting at the curb. Because my mother works, she couldn't volunteer to drive. My grandma takes care of me during the day, and she always takes the bus if she goes anywhere. Otherwise, she'd probably have volunteered, because she's a person who really likes to shop. She even has a sweatshirt that says: *Shop Till You Drop.*

I was hoping to go in Miss G.'s car. I thought it would be cool sitting next to her in the front seat. I would use my most polite, grown-up voice as we talked. Maybe she'd tell me all about how she never ate vegetables when she was little, either—although it was hard to imagine Miss G. ever being little!

Marsha's mother was driving the first car, so Marsha got to go with that group. The line moved forward, and before I knew it, I was sitting next to Matthew in the backseat of his mother's car.

"Wait!" I said. "I'm supposed to go with Miss G.!"

But Matthew's mother was busy checking seat belts and locking doors. I was trapped. She pulled the car away from the curb and started down the road to you-know-where, and I was sitting next to you-know-who. It was going to be a you-know-what kind of day.

Matthew was not happy about sitting next to me, either. I could guess that, because the first thing he said was, "Hey, Fish-Face! Don't get any cooties on me!" Matthew has called me Fish-Face ever since we were in kindergarten. Grandma said it was because he liked me. I think it was because I called him a doody head.

The five-minute drive felt like an hour. I had to make sure that my leg didn't touch Matthew's, and that took a lot of concentration.

Finally, we reached Shopper's Supreme, the neighborhood supermarket, which was about as exciting as a dead cat. Although I guess a dead cat could be an exciting thing if it was your pet and it died and you were really upset and you had a funeral for it.

"Please stay in line, and watch for cars!" Miss G. shouted as we walked across the parking lot.

My group followed Matthew's mother into the store. We all met by a corner booth with a sign that said MANAGER on it. A bald man in a white shirt with the sleeves rolled up waited until we were all quiet. He looked very familiar.

"Good morning, boys and girls!" the man

said loudly. "And welcome to Shopper's Supreme—the only store you need for all your shopping needs."

Now I knew who he was. He was Hank, the Shopper's Supreme man in the TV commercial. I, Annie Pitts, was standing in the same room with a famous person! I raised my hand.

"Are you really Hank, the Shopper's Supreme man on TV?" I asked.

"I certainly am, young lady," he answered. "And are you one of my loyal customers?"

"Oh, yes," I lied. "I do all my shopping in your store." Maybe if I sounded as if I really meant it, Hank would want me to be in one of his commercials. I would rather be in a regular TV show, but being in a commercial would be great, too, as long as it wasn't for underpants or something like that. That would be *so* embarrassing.

"Now *there's* a satisfied customer," Hank

said, pointing to me. "How would you like to be my helper?"

Would I! He actually asked me! He didn't ask Marsha-Miss-Teacher's-Pet-Who-Gets-Picked-All-the-Time. He asked me, Annie Pitts. I smiled and said in my best actress-like voice, "It would be your pleasure to have me."

Hank laughed and asked me to come forward. I stood next to him and smiled out at the class. Through my smiley teeth I tried to say, so only Hank could hear, "Just so you know, I don't do underwear commercials."

Hank gave me a funny look and handed me a huge poster to hold. On it was a diagram of the whole store. This was supposed to help us find all the different kinds of food.

Unfortunately, I was holding the poster in front of my face, so I couldn't see any of the diagram, but I did see Marsha taking lots of

notes. She was probably trying to impress Hank so that she could be in one of his commercials, too. She could be so obvious sometimes.

When he was finished, Hank wished us all good luck and reminded us to tell our parents that Shopper's Supreme was the only store they needed for all their shopping needs. I was left holding the poster, while the rest of the class headed for the aisles.

"Thank you, miss," Hank said, taking the poster. "You'd better catch up with the others." He gathered some important-looking papers and rushed past me. I guess he would talk to me later about my television career.

# Lettuce Begin

Miss G. had told us to stay with our groups, so I looked for Susan, Thomas, and Matthew. I found them in the fruits-and-vegetables aisle with Matthew's mother. They were running around, writing stuff down as if it were fun or something. I worked on my chart, too. I wrote APPLES under the fruit column. This was just too exciting for words.

Miss G. saw me. "There you are, Annie," she said. "I told everyone that I'm giving a point for each correct answer. We're trying to see who can get the most points."

Miss G. made it sound like a contest. Maybe the person with the most points would get a prize or something. Maybe it was the starring role in the school play! If that was it, I had some catching up to do.

Miss G. walked down the aisle saying, "Try to be creative. I'd like to see some unusual choices. The most interesting food names will get two points."

I checked my chart. Apples were definitely not a two-pointer. I looked around for something more interesting. I found persimmons and guavas.

Then I rushed across the aisle to the vegetables. As I said before, they were not my favorite kind of food, but maybe there were some unusual veggies worth two points. I had to weave my way around a lot of shopping carts to get there.

The store was getting very crowded, and I got trapped against a display bin, completely surrounded by shopping carts. Behind me was a huge pile of lettuce. I never thought of any vegetable as being very interesting, but lettuce had to be the dullest of them all. That is, until someone takes a head from the bottom of the pile and they all start to roll. Which is exactly what Matthew did. I suddenly found myself being attacked by hundreds of heads of iceberg lettuce!

Matthew's mother ran to help me up and apologized to the produce man, who did what he could to stop the rest of the lettuce from rolling. I would have offered to help, but I had more important work to do. I needed more points. I rushed through the bins, adding to my list: jicama, arugula, fennel, rutabaga, and taro—all worth at least three points each!

As my group made its way to the dairy

aisle, I kept my eyes open for Hank, in case he wanted to talk to me about any ideas I had for our commercial. I didn't see him anywhere, so I worked on my chart.

The dairy aisle was easy. I found weird stuff like goat cheese and soybean milk. As I waited for everyone else to finish, I practiced modeling with a container of strawberry yogurt. I held it up and smiled, pretending there was a camera in front of me. I picked up another yogurt—blueberry—and held it up also. I tried to see how long I could stand perfectly still and smile at the same time.

I was doing a really professional job, I thought, until I noticed that people were looking at me. That was okay. I would have to get used to that if I was going to be in commercials. Then I saw that they really were looking at Matthew, who was standing behind me, making faces.

I turned and my elbow hit his hand. I dropped a container of yogurt, and it splashed all over the floor and onto my shoes. There is nothing more disgusting than having blueberry yogurt oozing all over your white sneakers.

Fortunately, Hank wasn't around to see the mess I had made.

Unfortunately, Miss G. was. She mumbled something about aspirin, and handed me some tissues so that I could clean myself up. I hoped she would still let me be in the play after this. I would have to keep away from Matthew from now on, so I wouldn't get into any more trouble!

Just then, an announcement came over the loudspeaker: "Cleanup in the dairy aisle." It was Hank's voice.

As I raced away from the dairy aisle toward the meat department, I wondered if Hank actually saw me drop the yogurt, or if one of his workers reported that there was just a general mess on the floor, without mentioning the nine-year-old redhead who made it.

Suddenly, I found myself face-to-face with fish. Dozens of fish lying on a bed of ice. Actually, the fish were very interesting. They were shiny and scaly and had eyes that followed you when you walked past. But unfortunately Matthew couldn't resist saying, "Hey, Fish-Face! See any relatives here?"

And then it happened. Some strange person inside of me made me pick up one of the dead fish by the tail. That person also happened to fling the flounder straight at Matthew and smack him in the face.

Of course, I had nothing to do with it. It was that strange person inside of me. So you can imagine my surprise when Matthew started yelling at me. He didn't call me

Fish-Face, either. He used a word I had never heard before. It couldn't have been a very nice one, though, because his mother grabbed him by the arm and took him off to the side for a talk.

Miss G. remained somewhat calm. I thought that was very cool. Maybe she found her aspirin. She apologized to Hank, who had witnessed the whole ugly scene. That was not very cool. He politely asked us to leave his store; and before we knew it, we were being escorted to the exit.

I never found out what happened to the fish. It was last seen stretched out on the green linoleum of Shopper's Supreme. But its fate couldn't have been any worse than what was about to happen to me. Miss G. told me that I was to ride back with her group. And I don't think she wanted to talk about her childhood eating habits, either.

# The Story of Horace Tuttle

I always thought it would be special to ride in a teacher's car. The fact that I was about to get a lecture made it not so special. If only I hadn't flung that fish. . .

Miss G. cleared her throat as she pulled out of the parking lot. I sank lower into my seat and pretended I was admiring the treetops that whizzed past.

At the first red light, Miss G. finally spoke. But she didn't yell or anything like that.

She was actually quite nice. She said, "Annie, I know Matthew teases you and makes you angry sometimes. But you must try harder to control your reactions. If people took it upon themselves to solve their problems the way you did today, the world would be in a terrible mess."

I tried to imagine everyone in the whole world tossing fish around, and I had to agree with her. Things could get really messy. And smelly. My hand still smelled a little fishy. I wondered if Matthew's face smelled fishy, too.

Miss G. continued. "The rest of the class seems to be able to work nicely together. I just wish you could be a little less independent and follow directions like everyone else." She looked at me hopefully and said, "Can you give it a try, Annie?"

"Yes, Miss G.," I said. I really meant it, too.

Miss G. gave me a little smile, and I smiled

back. For the rest of the ride we were silent, but the kids in the backseat were laughing and fooling around. I guess they didn't think it was so special to be riding in a teacher's car.

When we reached the school, everyone rushed into the classroom, but Miss G. called me back into the hall. Uh-oh, I thought. Now that we're alone, she's really going to let me have it. But what she said surprised me.

"You know, Annie," she began. "When I was your age, there was a boy in my class who teased me so much that I finally had to do something. Something bad. I knew I wasn't a bad person, but something inside of me had to do something bad to Horace Tuttle."

My jaw dropped. "What did you do to Horace Tuttle?" I dared to ask.

"I glued his math book shut," she said quite casually.

I gasped. My own teacher had done what she always told us not to do. We were not to treat a book unkindly. If we made a pencil mark in our books, we were being "unkind." Imagine globbing glue between the pages! That would be like murdering it! I stared at her as if she were suddenly from another planet.

Miss G. went on. "Even though I paid for the book, my teacher made it clear that she was disappointed in me. Maybe that's why I'm such a 'clean book' fanatic today!"

Miss G. chuckled a little, but I didn't think it was funny. I hoped she wasn't disappointed in me. Maybe I should offer to pay for the fish. Or maybe I could buy some special shampoo that would get the smell out of Matthew's hair. Finally, I decided that I should just try harder to stay out of trouble.

Once we were back in the classroom,

Miss G. acted like she always did. She was very good at pretending that she was a normal teacher and not an ex–book murderer. She could probably be an actress someday if she really wanted to. I would be sure to suggest it to her when I got a chance. I could even help her practice smiling.

We spent the rest of the afternoon reviewing proper trip behavior. Again. I thought that the play would be canceled because some of us acted so poorly. That would mean no play and no commercial. I could see that my acting career was off to a pretty slow start!

So I was surprised when Miss G. announced that the play would go on as planned. "Maybe we shouldn't," she said, "but this is the last chance for you to show me that you really can work together."

She was looking at Matthew and me when she said that.

I was very good for the rest of the day, which was about ten more minutes. I didn't even laugh when Matthew tripped on his way to the board. The rest of the poorly behaved class did, but not me. I sat perfectly still with my hands folded on my desk. I was so good for so long that I almost exploded by the time the bell rang.

When I got home, I told Grandma all about the trip and how I got into trouble. She wasn't upset with me, and she wasn't upset about Miss G. being a book killer. Instead she just smiled whenever I mentioned Matthew's name.

"I remember a boy who always teased me when I was in school," she said.

"Was his name Horace Tuttle, by any chance?" I asked.

"No, I called him Silly Willy."

"Did you do something bad to Silly Willy?" I asked.

"I married him." She laughed. "Your grandpa William wouldn't leave me alone until I did!"

My grandpa died a couple of years ago. But all the time I knew him, he was always playing jokes on my grandma. She seemed to like it, though. Once, he painted black cow spots on her white sneakers, because she collected cow figures. She actually thought it was neat, and and she still wears those sneakers, even though they're really old and worn out.

All of this wasn't helping me much. I wasn't about to marry Matthew, or glue his books shut. I would have to deal with him in my own way. But I would have to think about that later. Right now I wanted to concentrate on the school play. Miss G. had asked us to think about ideas for it.

I had thought of a really great idea. I could

be a TV chef who shows viewers how to make fancy stuff like wedding cakes. Only I would make healthy stuff like whole wheat wedding cakes. The rest of the class would be the camera crew, except for Marsha-Miss-Never-Touch-Dirt. I would make her clean up the kitchen after me.

The next day we discussed our ideas in class. Miss G. listed three of our best ideas on the board, including mine about the TV chef. I was sure my idea was the best. It was far superior to Matthew's idea about killer tomatoes eating people, and Marsha's idea about a cook finding a magic kettle.

We raised our hands to vote for our favorite. To my surprise, Marsha-Miss-I-Won-I-Won got the most votes. Things went downhill from there.

Miss G. listed all the parts on the board so that the kids could choose their roles. Due to the unfortunate fish incident at Shopper's

Supreme, Miss G. said that Matthew and I would be the last to choose.

But I couldn't complain. I was just happy she let us be in the play at all.

Of course, Marsha-Miss-Wonderful got the leading role as the cook, because the story was her idea. One by one, everyone picked a part. The junk foods were very popular. Susan picked the part of the Twinkie, and Elan chose the chocolate bar. Some of the other junk foods were ice cream, peppermint candy, and my own personal favorite, jelly beans. Patty took that part. I was so jealous.

When there were no more junk-food parts left, the class took turns choosing the more healthy foods. Thomas chose the part of the apple, but then insisted that it be changed to grapes. He had seen a really cool grapes costume in a catalog, and he was sure his mother would order it for him.

Miss G. did say that our parents could help

us with our costumes. I guess that's a form of helping, if your parents order a costume from a catalog for you, but I was sure my grandma would help me make one that was just as special.

When there were only two parts remaining, Matthew chose the granola, and I got the one that was left. I, Annie Pitts, was the artichoke.

# Too Many Cooks

The Cook and the Magic Kettle" was about a cook who finds a magic pot that gives her whatever food she wishes for. At first, the cook wants only sweets. Each time she wishes for something sweet, a kid dressed up as a junk food would pop up out of the pot and say his lines. Then the cook pretends to eat him.

Of course, all that bad food makes the cook sick, so she wishes for good foods like vegetables and dairy products. After she eats them, she becomes healthy again. In our grand finale, we sing a song about the joys of a healthy body. This had to be the worst idea for a play I ever heard of!

Since Marsha got the part of the cook, she acted as if she were the queen of the world. She would refer to me as "that vegetable." She would whine to Miss G., "Does that vegetable have to stand in front of me? No one can see me." Or she would say things like, "Does that vegetable have to say her lines so loud? No one can hear me."

I had to listen to this every day when we rehearsed at recess. But mostly I stood around and watched, because the artichoke didn't really have much to say. My lines were:

*Eat your veggies every day.*
*They're full of fiber and vitamin A.*

That was it. After a couple of days, I knew everyone else's part, too. When Thomas was sick on Thursday, I filled in for him during the rehearsal. When Patty was absent on Friday, Miss G. asked me to say her lines also.

I was so good at remembering everyone's lines that Miss G. asked me to fill in for anyone who was absent during the actual play.

"No problem," I answered. The truth was, any part was better than the artichoke. Except maybe for Jamie's part. He was the fish.

Meanwhile, I watched Marsha for any signs of a cold or the flu. I would be ready! Every now and then, I would walk up to her and say, "You look pale, Marsha. Are you sure you're feeling okay? Maybe you should see the nurse."

After lunch, I would say things like, "I hope you didn't eat that tuna fish sandwich,

Marsha. I ate tuna fish just like that last week, and it made me throw up."

But Marsha paid no attention to me. She went right on being healthy. But I still watched. And waited.

A week before the play, Grandma helped me with my costume. Mom bought an artichoke so that we could see how it was put together. I thought it was put together rather strangely. It didn't really look like food, but more like a cactus plant. I wondered what would have made someone think that it was edible. I mean, did a caveman accidentally put one in his mouth and say, "Food," and from then on people knew that they could eat artichokes?

These mind-boggling thoughts didn't bother Grandma. She just started right in on the costume. I helped her cut giant leaves out of green felt. Then she sewed them onto my

Halloween pumpkin costume that she had made for me last year. It was just the right shape for an artichoke.

I stood in front of the big mirror in my mother's room with the costume on.

I was a pretty cute artichoke, if I do say so myself. I turned around slowly, trying to see myself as the audience would. If I had to be an artichoke, I was going to be the best one I could be! I practiced smiling and bowing. Bowing took more practice, because it wasn't easy to bend if you were a big, puffy vegetable.

I practiced my lines over and over:

> *Eat your veggies every day.*
> *They're full of fiber and vitamin A.*

I practiced each word as loudly and as clearly as I could. I shouted out loud, "Fiber, fiber, FIBER!"

Mom came running into the room, screaming, "Oh, my God! Where's the fire?"

"Not 'fire,'" I said. "'Fiber.' Veggies are full of it." I guess I needed to work more on my pronunciation.

That night Mom cooked the artichoke. The real one, not the costume. But of course I didn't eat it.

# Play Time!

Mom arranged to take off from work on the afternoon of the play. I was glad, because she doesn't get to visit my school very often like some of the parents who don't work during the day. Grandma was coming, too.

When I got to school, I hung up my costume and took a quick look to see who was absent. Marsha showed up. Looking well, I might add. But Jamie was home sick. Great. Besides being the artichoke, I would have the honor of playing the part of the fish.

Of course, I knew what Matthew was thinking. He said it out loud. "Hey, Fish-Face. You should be really good at Jamie's part. You won't even have to act!"

But I wasn't going to let anything spoil my acting career today, not even Matthew. I tossed my hair and said, "You're such a child, Matthew." Then I turned and left in my most actress-like way. No, Matthew was no longer a bother. I had more important things to do. I was Annie Pitts, artichoke. And fish.

After lunch, we got into our costumes and waited in the classroom while the rest of the school and the parents filled the auditorium. We were unusually quiet. Even Matthew. If I didn't know better, I would say that he was nervous.

Miss G. stood in the front of the room wearing a new dress she probably had bought just for the play. She had lost some weight these past few weeks, and we were very, very proud of her. It must have been hard for her to rehearse every day with talking food!

When she had our attention, she said, "Boys and girls, you've worked very hard together these past weeks. I think this will be the best play my class has ever done! Now, let's move quietly to the stage, just like we practiced." I could tell that she was proud of us, too.

We marched down the hall as quietly as we could. It was hard because some of the costumes made swishing and clacking noises when we walked. Besides wearing my artichoke costume, I carried the large cardboard fish that Jamie had made. I was supposed to hold it in front of me when I said his lines.

When we went through the back door of the stage, the curtain was closed and we took our places. Marsha-Miss-Aren't-I-Lucky-to-Be-the-

Star-of-the-School-Play stood in the center. The big cardboard kettle was on the left side of the stage, right next to the curtain.

As she "wished" for each food, the kid was supposed to pop up from behind the pot to say his lines. Then they were to line up neatly across the center of the stage in preparation for the grand finale.

Miss G. gave the signal and the curtain opened. There was some applause from the audience. Then Marsha-the-Worst-Actress-in-the-World strolled across the stage and pretended to find the humongous kettle in the middle of the woods. She read the note attached to it:

> *Be it sweet, or be it meat;*
> *whatever you wish, you'll get to eat.*

She wished for some chocolate, and a giant candy bar popped out of the pot. Elan said his part, then walked to his place to start the line of foods.

One by one, the rest of the junk foods popped out of the pot after the cook wished for them, and the audience applauded after each speech. So far, so good.

The Twinkie was the last sweet food that the cook wished for. Susan was dressed in her yellow ballet tights and leotard, and had a piece of plastic wrapped around her. She looked just like a real package of Twinkies because she had drawn the label on the front. She popped up and said:

> *Sugar is good, and sugar is sweet;*
> *but before you know it, you'll have no teeth.*

Marsha pretended to take a bite out of the Twinkie and said, "Yum." After she was "eaten," the Twinkie took the most

elegant bow I'd ever seen. Then she twirled and twirled across the stage to her place in line.

That wasn't the way we rehearsed it, but Susan has been taking ballet lessons since she was four. I guess she just automatically twirls and bows when she gets in front of an audience. The audience applauded loudly. When they quieted down, Marsha said her lines. She held her stomach and shouted:

> *That's enough of this bad food!*
> *I need a meal that's healthy and good.*

My turn, I mean Jamie's turn, was next. I held the fish in front of me and popped up from behind the pot. I said his lines perfectly:

> *Protein makes your muscles strong.*
> *I'm brain food, too, so I can't be wrong.*

I walked across the stage, peeking out from behind the fish so that everyone would know that it was me, not Jamie. When the audience applauded, they applauded for Annie Pitts, so of course I took an elegant bow, just as Susan had done. I can't describe the feeling I had as I bowed again and again. And again. Maybe next time I'd try spinning, too.

# The

# Grand Finale

I ducked behind the curtain and crossed the stage so that I could pop up again as the artichoke. Before I left, though, I noticed the video camera that was standing in the center aisle. Our show was being taped! I was going to be in a movie!

I got so excited that I bumped into Miss G. behind the curtain. "There's a video camera out there!" I said in a loud whisper.

"I know," she whispered back. "The principal said he would make copies of the play for the parents who wanted to buy one. Now hurry back in line." She scooted me behind Matthew. It was almost his turn.

"They're taping the play," I whispered to him. "We're going to be in a movie!"

Matthew wasn't excited. Matthew wasn't even moving. Marsha motioned for him to come out from behind the curtain when it was his turn, but he just wouldn't budge. "I forgot my lines!" he squeaked.

I didn't want Matthew to ruin the play, so I said, "Don't worry, I'll whisper them to you. Now get behind the kettle!" That seemed to do the trick, because Matthew slowly made his way over to the pot.

Unfortunately, he couldn't bend very well in the granola box. He had trouble hiding behind the pot. His head was still sticking up when Marsha was supposed to say her lines. Instead of her lines, she said, "Get down, Matthew. Everyone can see you!"

There were some giggles from the audience, but Matthew still couldn't bend low enough.

So Marsha took matters into her own hands. She pressed down on Matthew's shoulders, hoping to bend the box. Instead, Matthew lost his balance and fell over backward, taking the cardboard kettle with him. He landed flat on his back and was stuck there, like an upside-down turtle.

But the fall must have jolted his memory, because it was at this awkward moment that Matthew suddenly remembered his lines. And from the fallen granola box, we heard:

*Grains like wheat and corn and rice*
*stand tall and straight and taste so nice.*

The audience was roaring with laughter by now, especially the older kids. The teachers couldn't quiet them. I actually felt sorry for

Matthew. I'm sure his parents were out there watching.

Other than Marsha, I was the one standing the closest to him. I marched very matter-of-factly over to Matthew and helped him get up. Then I helped Marsha set the kettle back up. In the middle of the laughter, some kids started applauding, so I bowed politely once and returned to my place behind the curtain.

The artichoke was the last one to go on, and I think everyone, especially Marsha, couldn't wait for the play to end. She really wasn't handling this very well. As for me, I thought it was fun. I was looking forward to my big moment.

I popped up from behind the kettle, but before I spoke, I gave one of my biggest smiles. I was so glad I spent all that time practicing. As I smiled, I looked at all the faces to see if I could see Mom and Grandma. I couldn't find them, but I did see someone I knew right down in the front row. It was Hank! He must have been interested in my acting after all. This was so exciting!

I cleared my throat and said loudly:

> *Eat your veggies every day.*
> *They're full of fire and vitamin A.*

Then I twirled and twirled to the front of the stage just like Susan did. This was not hard at all, I decided. As I spun in front of the line of kids, I thought I heard a snicker. Then a giggle. As I spun past Thomas, I was sure I heard him say, "She said it wrong!"

Was that possible? Could I, Annie Pitts, star of stage, say my lines wrong? I went over the words in my head as I continued to spin. I had said:

*Eat your veggies every day.*
*They're full of fire and vitamin A.*

Fire? I said *fire*? At that very instant, I realized my mistake. At that very instant, I also
spun right into granola Matthew, knocking
him into Thomas, the bunch of grapes, who
of course fell on top of Ayuko, the milk bot-
tle, who then rammed into Gregory, the blob
of spaghetti, squishing him into Max, the
egg, making him trip over Maria, the banana.
It continued like this right on down the line.

Pinned under Matthew, I couldn't get up,
but I could see everyone fall, one by one, just
like dominoes, only in slow motion.

When the final chocolate bar had fallen, the
only one left standing was Marsha-Miss-Do-
the-Right-Thing. She was holding the sign
that said GRAND FINALE just like she was
supposed to do. The last thing we heard was

the audience laughing and Miss G. yelling, "Curtain, curtain!"

When the curtain closed, we all struggled to get up for the final song. This took a while, but the audience was laughing and clapping the whole time. I never felt so humiliated in my entire life. I, Annie Pitts, had ruined the play.

And here I was standing next to, of all people, Matthew. I didn't want to hear what he had to say about my performance. Whatever it was, I deserved it. But he surprised me when he whispered, "Wasn't that awesome! Everyone crashing all over the place? Annie, you were great!"

I didn't agree with him, but I thought that was a compliment, so I said, "Thanks." I also think I heard him call me Annie, not Fish-Face, so I said, "Thanks" again. Maybe my Matthew problem was finally over.

When we were somewhat in order, Miss G. stood in the center of the line. The curtain opened, and we sang our grand finale. We sang about bones and blood and muscles and teeth. It was a gross song, actually, but there we were, singing our little hearts out. Well, if the show must go on, then I would go with it. I sang every verse without a single mistake.

When the song was over, we all bowed. Except for Matthew. He wasn't taking any chances this time. The audience cheered and clapped. Hank jumped up from his seat and handed Miss G. a bouquet of flowers. I thought that was *so* theatrical!

When the curtain finally closed, everyone marched happily off the stage. Miss G. caught up with me. She put her arm around me and said, "Annie, I want to thank you for helping Matthew. Now that's what I call working together."

"But I messed up the play," I said.

"No, you didn't," she said. "You didn't follow directions, but sometimes a surprise or two is a good thing. That's why I enjoy having you in my class." That was two compliments in one afternoon! I guess my mistake wasn't that bad after all.

Then she gave me a hug. A teacher hug is one of the best kinds, and I, Annie Pitts, got a teacher hug that afternoon.

# Where's the Bug Juice?

After we changed out of our costumes, we met our families in the gym for refreshments. There was a table full of food with little cards attached to the plates and bowls listing the ingredients for each dish. My idea of refreshments is bug juice and Rice Krispies Treats. But Miss G. felt that nutritious treats would be more appropriate. There were cut-up vegetables, a spinach pie, all kinds of cheeses, whole-grain bread, and some things that I had never heard of before, like tabouli and couscous.

I found Mom and Grandma at the end of the table, piling the stuff onto their plates. Mom gave me a squeeze and said, "Great play, honey. You really brought the house down!"

"I guess I did, didn't I," I said, laughing.

"I hope you aren't upset," Mom continued. "I'm sure every great actress has made a mistake or two. But it shouldn't discourage you."

I knew Mom was trying to cheer me up, but I really didn't feel so bad. I wasn't going to let one little mistake stop me. I was still serious about becoming a real actress. In fact, I would go right up to Hank and tell him I was ready to be in his commercial. I'd show everybody how serious I really was!

I looked around the room for any sign of

Hank. I didn't see him, but I did spot Matthew heading my way. He was munching on a rice cake, and the little pieces were falling all over his shirt.

Between bites, he said, "You know, this play turned out okay, but my brother and I make much better stuff. We make up stories for monster movies. Then we videotape them. He does most of the shooting, and I play the monsters. I even get to carry around a fake head sometimes. He's got some great ideas."

I was surprised to hear all this. "I thought you got stage fright," I said.

"I don't like to get up in front of a hundred people! But I think it's fun to make monster movies. Besides, you can always cut out the mistakes."

"You mean, like my little accident?" I asked.

"No way! That was the best part." Matthew laughed and pretended he was me, spinning. A rather poor imitation, I thought.

"Anyway," he continued, "my brother says we need to get some more actors. If you want, you can be the Swamp Monster, or something like that."

Matthew waited for me to say something, but I didn't know what to say. Sara and I always made up plays about brave princesses and wizards. But I guess an actress shouldn't be too fussy about what parts to play when she's just starting.

So I said, "Okay."

"Great!" Matthew said. "I'll tell my brother." Then he headed back to the food table.

"Such a nice young man," Grandma said after he left. "That was Matthew, wasn't it?"

"Yes, that's Matthew," I admitted.

"The same Matthew you smacked with a dead fish?"

"He asked me if I wanted to be in his monster video. I said I would. Is that okay?"

Grandma looked very serious and said, "It wouldn't involve dead fish, would it?"

"I don't think so," I answered. "Maybe just some guts and stuff."

"Sounds lovely," Grandma said. "But I've suddenly lost my appetite. Perhaps you'll finish this for me." She handed me a plate of greenish stuff.

"What is it?" I asked. I wasn't about to eat something that strange-looking without asking.

"Artichoke hearts," she answered.

I was poking around the green stuff when Miss G. came over. "Try it, Annie," she said. "It's so delicious."

"And fresh, too!" A familiar voice boomed from behind her. It was Hank. "Say, speaking of artichokes, weren't you the one who spun out of control today? Ho, ho, ho!" He was, of course, impressed by my performance.

"I was," I admitted. Then I smiled one of my practiced smiles. I was hoping he wouldn't ask if I was also the kid who flung the flounder at Shopper's Supreme.

At this point, I expected Hank to ask about my being in a commercial, so I said,"Is there something you'd like to say?"

"Why, yes," he said with great enthusiasm.

He stepped to the front of the room to make an announcement. This was it, I thought. He's going to tell everyone that I've been chosen to be in his commercial!

"May I have your attention, please!" he shouted.

I didn't expect him to be so dramatic, but he was, after all, an actor.

When everyone was quiet, Hank made his speech. "I'd like to remind everyone that all this food was donated by Shopper's Supreme— the only store you need for all your shopping needs! Our catering and take-out departments are open at seven a.m. for your convenience."

Supermarkets? Why is he talking about supermarkets, I wondered. Hank turned and walked back to the food table, while I tried to figure out what had just happened.

Miss G. giggled and said, "Isn't he wonderful to do all this? I invited him to the play, and this is what he did!"

I finally realized that Hank wasn't here to see me. He was here for Miss G. "You invited him?" I asked.

"Oh, yes," Miss G. said. "We've been dating ever since we met that day at the supermarket. We have so much in common. We're both interested in nutrition, and we both retire soon. Hank's already talking about opening a health spa together! We'll call it Ranch Rutabaga."

So that was it. I wasn't going to be in a

commercial after all. Maybe Miss G. will be in one. I can picture her and Hank together. She can hold up the yogurt and smile, while Hank announces the flavor of the week.

That was okay. I did have another offer. I would be Annie Pitts, Swamp Monster. Besides, I already had a green scaly costume. And those artichoke hearts would make terrific guts. . . .